THE AUTHOR

Lisa Dennis is the wife of Ron, Team Principal of the McLaren Formula One team. She loves travelling the world, attending all the races. Her many amazing experiences – and her own inventive children – have inspired her to create Mac & Lauren.

LISA DENNIS

MAC & LAUREN ™

FAIR PLAY!

SUZUKA
RACE CIRCUIT

JAPAN

Circuit Length:
3.644 Miles (4.19km)

POCKET BOOKS

An imprint of Simon & Schuster UK Ltd. Africa House, 64-78 Kingsway, London WC2B 6AH
A Viacom Company
First published in Great Britain by Simon & Schuster UK Ltd
This book is copyright under the Berne Convention
No reproduction without permission
Text copyright © Lisa Dennis 2002
Illustrations by Red Giraffe © Simon & Schuster 2002
All rights reserved
Pocket Books & colophon are registered trademarks of Simon & Schuster
A CIP catalogue record for this book is available from the British Library
ISBN 07434 5054X
1 3 5 7 9 10 8 6 4 2

'I can't wait to get off this plane and have some fun,' yawned Mac.

'Too right!' Lauren agreed. 'Fourteen hours crammed in with all these spare parts is a long time to sit still!'

'As soon as we land in Japan, the first race will be to the funfair to burn off some energy!' laughed Lucky.

'And that will be just the first race I win this weekend,' bragged Bruno.

At the airport, Bruno barged through the gates, pushing the surprised fans out of the way.

'Race you to the dodgems, Maddy!' revved Bruno as they squealed in opposite directions around the funfair.

But Bruno took a corner too fast, and knocked into a refreshments stall. He skidded to a halt in a mountain of popcorn!

'Look, it's our hero, Bruno!' rumbled a little car from the kiddy-racers track. Soon Bruno was surrounded by tiny go-karts.

'My name's Sumo,' said the littlest car of all. 'I want to be just like you when I grow up, Bruno. I'd do anything to be a real racing car!'

'Who cares?' grumbled Bruno rudely. Then a thought struck him. 'Hang on. Maybe there is something you can help me with. Did you know that proper racing cars all carry a special tracker that the timers use to record our lap times? It's called a transponder…'

Sumo nodded, and Bruno whispered his plan…

On the other side of the park, the other cars queued for the strongman stall. Franco had rung the bell and was posing for photographs. But Marco was sulking because he could only get the strength-marker half way up.

'Maybe you should ask the wishing wall in Kyoto for some more power,' said Lauren.

'Yes,' said Mac. 'It's like making a wish when you blow out the candles on your birthday cake. Sometimes, they come true!'

'I'm going to wish that I win the race!' decided Marco.

'No,' said Franco. 'You're going to wish that **I** win, because I'm older than you!'

'Ha!' Marco revved. 'We'll see about that!'

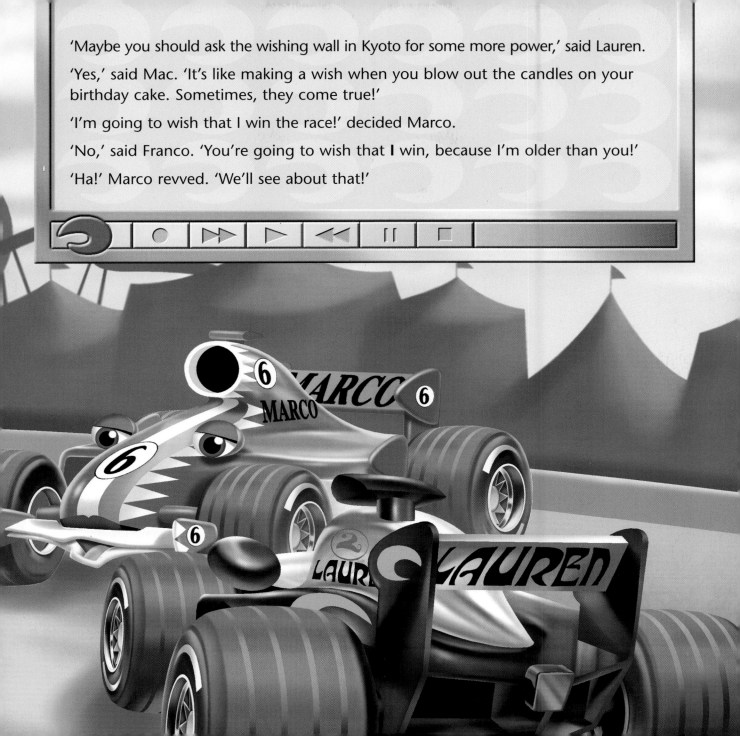

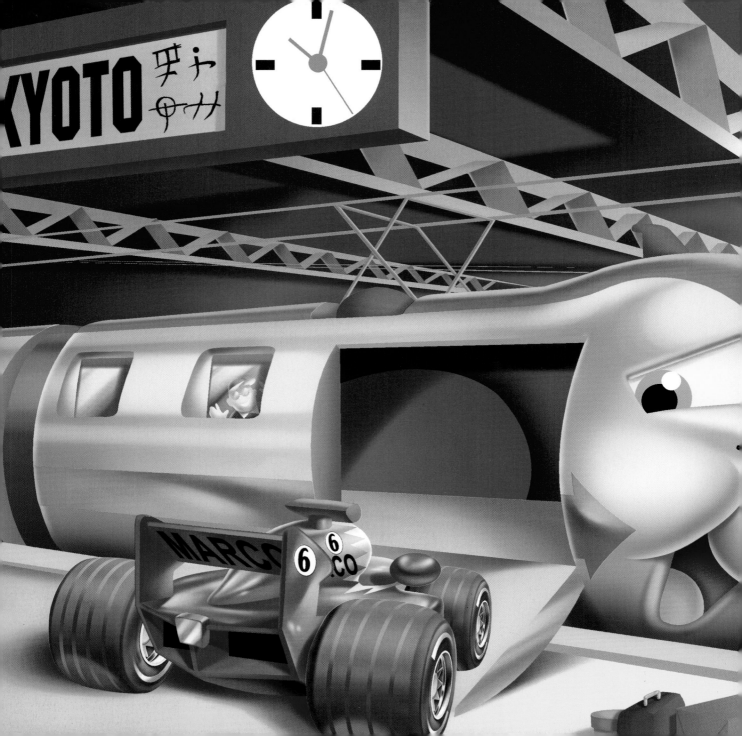

Maddy wanted to make some trouble.

'Franco, give Marco the wrong train times for getting back,' she suggested sweetly. 'Then he'll be late for qualifying and his wish can't come true!'

'Great idea,' growled Franco. Soon, Marco was off on the bullet train, not realising he would miss the the race completely!

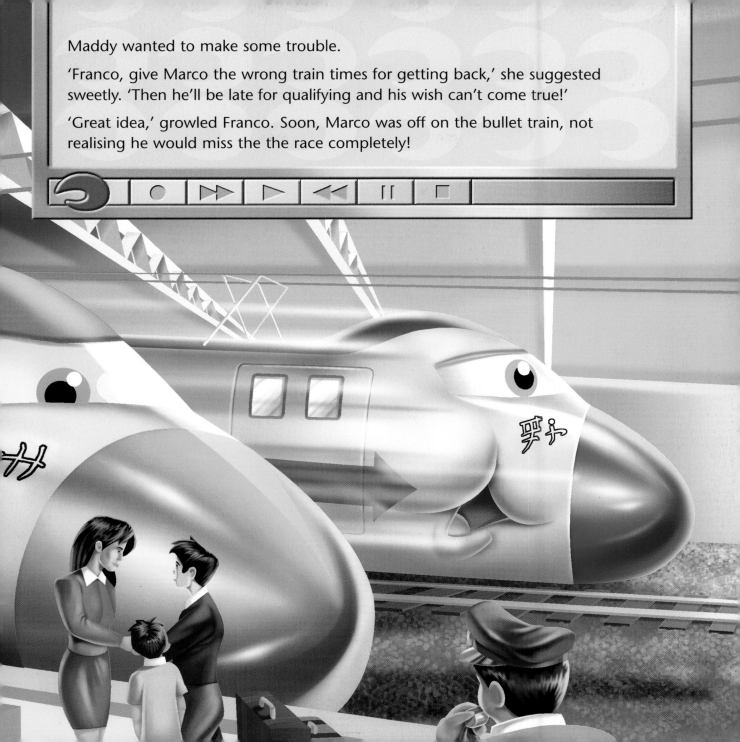

Sumo was so excited to be helping his hero that he turned up early on Sunday morning, ready for the race. He was so little that nobody noticed him trundle into Bruno's pits.

Bruno was talking to Computer. 'I've tricked this stupid kiddy car into doing something naughty for me!'

'Nice one, Bruno,' crackled Computer. 'And if the little car gets caught, we'll pretend we never met him!'

Little Sumo slipped away miserably.

'Why are you looking so sad?' Lauren asked Sumo as he passed by.

Sumo blushed. 'Oh, er – nothing. I'm just fed up.'

'Would you like to help us?' Mac asked. 'I'm sure we can find you something to do that will take your mind off your troubles. You can be part of our team!'

Little Sumo had never been happier. He carried spanners to and fro and talked to Mac and Lauren about his dreams of becoming a real racing car.

'If you practice really hard, and play by the rules, anything is possible,' Mac told him.

Sumo decided on a plan of his own. He said goodbye to his new friends and raced down to Bruno's garage.

'Where have you been?' roared Bruno. 'You'll never be a racing car if you don't do what I tell you! Now, get to the finish line. You know what to do…'

'You bet I do!' agreed Sumo, as he rushed away.

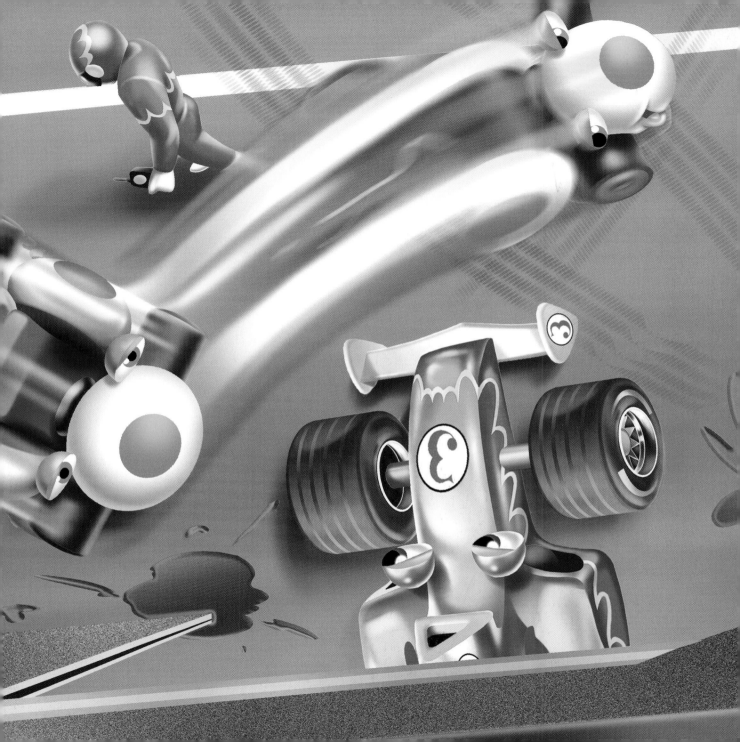

'1,2,3,4,5 - **Lights out!**' The race began.

Sumo cowered by the side of the track as the powerful cars roared past. 'This is scary,' he thought. 'Not like my peaceful go-kart track!'

Each lap of the race, Franco went more slowly. 'I wish I hadn't tricked Marco,' he thought guiltily. 'Where is he now?'

Maddy – who didn't care at all about the missing Marco – was flying around the circuit. She was just about to lap Franco when he pulled out to overtake Lucky – and bumped into her **HARD**.

'**Whoooooaaaaaa!**' squealed Franco as he went into a spin.

'That's not fair!' Maddy shouted as she smashed out of control.

'I guess nobody asked the wishing wall for either of us to win,' said Franco.

The race carried on, faster and faster. Little Sumo was still crouched down by the track, covered with burnt rubber and dust. He was shaking with fright.

On the last lap, Mac was leading the race with Bruno close behind. As they came around the bend, Bruno shot his transponder over to Sumo. 'Whoever's in the lead, just drive across the finish line ahead of them so that my transponder crosses first!' Bruno roared.

'Sure thing,' said Sumo as he drove off – in the opposite direction! 'Tricksters deserve to finish last!' he chuckled.

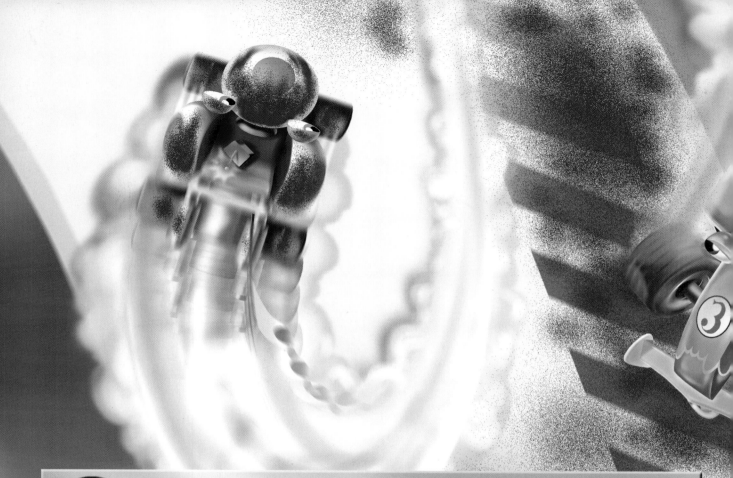

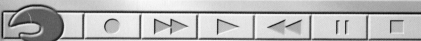

Mac and Lauren were surprised to see little Sumo as they drove across the finish line in first and second place.

When Bruno saw that he had finished last in the race, he was so angry he went red in the paintwork.

'I'll get you, pipsqueak!' roared Bruno as he chased after Sumo, who was hurrying back to the safety of the funfair.

'Quick, Mac!' shouted Lauren. 'We've got to help our little team-mate!'

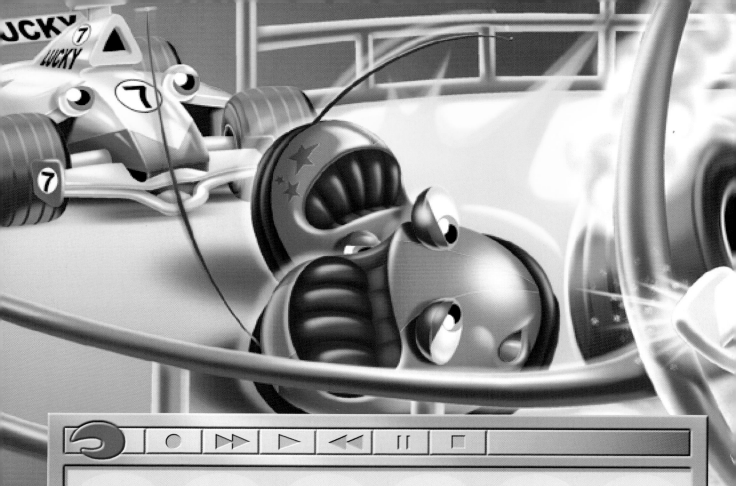

They raced after Bruno, and all the other cars followed too.

'I'll hide on the dodgems,' gasped Sumo as he raced up the ramp.

But it was too late. Bruno roared up behind him! Then Sumo slid down the little ramp on the other side – but Bruno was too big to fit.

'I guess this is one time you wish you were a little car too!' teased Sumo as all the other dodgem cars crashed into Bruno, again and again.

'**Ow!**' he yelled. '**Get off!**'

'This is just the place for you, Bruno,' laughed Lucky. 'No rules, and lots of bullying!'

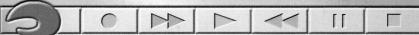

All the cars went off to celebrate Mac's victory at the big wheel. As they were waiting in the queue, Marco turned up.

'I couldn't decide who to wish for, so I wished that the best car should win,' said Marco.

'Your wish came true then,' agreed all the other cars as they cheered Mac, the race winner. 'The best car **did** win!'

And, staring out over Japan from high up on the big wheel, Mac and Lauren really did feel like they were on top of the world!